To Steve and Val and their flock

Text and illustrations © Rob Lewis 1987

First published in Great Britain in 1987
by Macdonald & Co (publishers) Ltd

This edition published in 1999
by Macdonald Young Books
an imprint of Wayland Publishers Ltd
61 Western Road
Hove
East Sussex
BN3 1JD

Find Macdonald Young Books on the Internet at
http://www.myb.co.uk

Printed and bound in Belgium by Proost International Book Production

British Library Cataloguing in Publication Data available

ISBN: 0 7500 2919 6

Friska
the sheep that was too small

written and illustrated by
Rob Lewis

MACDONALD YOUNG BOOKS

One bright spring morning,
Friska was born.

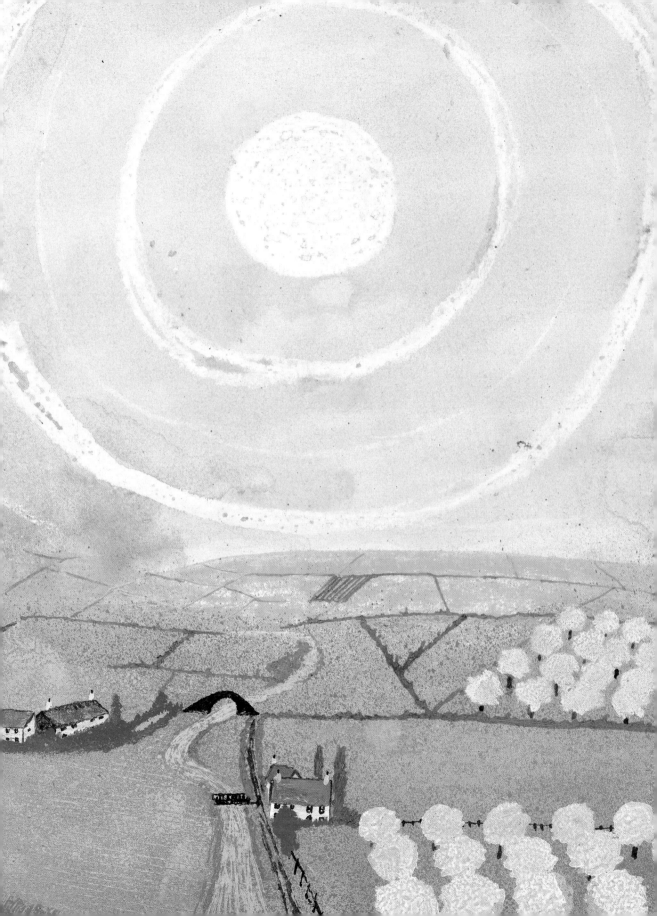

All year the other lambs grew,
but Friska stayed the same size.
She was a very small sheep.

All the sheep laughed at her
because she was so small.
This made her very unhappy.

To make herself look big,
she covered herself with snow.

But when spring came,
the snow all melted.

She let the white cherry blossom fall on her.

But a strong wind blew it all away.

She stole a fleece from the shepherds
at shearing time.

But one of the shepherds noticed,
and took it back.

Then one evening
a fierce wolf spied the flock of sheep
and thought what a tasty meal they'd make.

He chased the sheep until
they were too tired to run any further,
and then he prepared to pounce.
He didn't see Friska because
she was so small.

She bravely crept up behind the wolf
and bit his tail hard. Chomp!
The wolf let out a dreadful howl.
'Aaaaeee!'

'A monster has got me!
Let me go, kind monster,
and I will never come back again!'

So Friska let go – but she hid behind a bush
in case it was a trick.

But the wolf ran off into the forest.
He didn't dare to look back at
the terrible monster.

Friska had saved the sheep
and she was never laughed at again.